My Summer At The Lighthouse

A Boy's Journal

By Frederick Stonehouse

Illustrated by Susan Alby Meyer

©2003 Avery Color Studios, Inc.

ISBN: 1-892384-18-3

Library of Congress Control Number: 2002113371

First Edition 2003

Published by
Avery Color Studios, Inc.
511 D Avenue
Gwinn, Michigan 49841

Call 1-800-722-9925
for a catalog of other products.

"Look Johnny. Look out there!"

I stared out into the storm whipped water, following my Grandpa's direction. A big steam ship was fighting her way through the raging storm. Huge gray waves rolled over her but each time she shook them off like a wet dog and kept going. Jagged lightning flashed across the dark sky quickly followed by the deafening rumble of thunder.

"The waves are too big," I said. "That ship will never make it! She will sink and all the people will drown!"

"No Johnny," my Grandpa said. "The shipyard built her strong and she will survive this gale and many more, as long as her captain can see our light to keep clear of Ripper Rocks." He turned and looked over his shoulder at the big lens behind us.

Just then a shower of hail rattled loudly into the lantern room windows and a powerful blast of wind shook the tower. "Has a light tower ever blown down in a storm?" I asked him. "Aye lad they have, but this one never will. I helped build it so I ought to know."

"Johnny, Johnny, are you listening to me? Did you hear a single word I said?"

"Yes, Miss Swenson." I blurted out. "I heard everything you said. You were talking about, er, ah, I guess I just forgot?" My teacher was right. I had been daydreaming about a storm my Grandpa and I watched from his lighthouse tower last year. It was more exciting than listening to old Miss Swenson! She is just an old maid school teacher. What does she know?

"Johnny, you stop your daydreaming and listen to me! This is very important." Miss Swenson glared at me as she said, "Class, as I said, I want each of you to keep a journal of everything that you do during your summer vacation. Next fall when school starts again we will read them in class and learn all about your summer adventures."

I thought, "That's a waste of time. What a lame thing to do during the summer. I will not have any fun at all!"

June 16

Dear Journal,

   Hi, my name is Johnny and
my Grandpa is a lighthouse keeper.
The only reason I am keeping this
journal is because my teacher said I had to.
She said all of her students had to keep a
journal of their summer "adventures." I don't know
about the adventure part, but I will do my best anyway.

   I am 12 years old and this is the first year my parents allowed me to stay at
the lighthouse all summer without my brothers or sisters! I always enjoy it
when I visit my Grandpa and staying the whole summer will be great fun.

   Grandpa said I would work as his assistant keeper since his real assistant
would be gone most of the summer helping at another lighthouse. He said he
will teach me everything I need to know, but I remember some things from
last year's visit so learning it all will not be too hard.

   I arrived at the lighthouse today and it is just like I remembered from last
year. When I called it a lighthouse, Grandpa corrected me and said, "If you are
going to be my assistant, then you have to call it by the right name. This is
really a light ***station***."

We have more than just a lighthouse. The house we live in is really called the keeper's quarters. Next to the light tower is a small brick building that we store the oil in. Grandpa said this was important since if the oil ever caught fire, the little brick house would not burn. There are two buildings down by the water. One is called the fog house. When I was little I thought this was where Grandpa kept fog! Now I know better. Inside are two big steam powered horns that blow when the fog gets thick. There are also two big boilers and Grandpa has to start a coal fire under them to get the steam up, then an automatic mechanism blows each horn in turn. They are really loud!

Grandpa said ships can hear them over five miles away. When the sailors hear the horns, they know to stay away from our light.

The other building near the water is the boathouse. It contains the station sailboat. Grandpa uses it when he has to go to town for supplies. Sometimes he takes me fishing in it too. A long wooden dock goes from the boathouse out into the water. This is where supply boats from the big lighthouse tenders dock. But I will tell you more about that later.

The last building is the smallest of all, but also the most important. Grandpa calls it the "necessary house." At home we call it the outhouse.

June 17

Today Grandpa took me up to the lens room right at the top of the tower. I had been there last year but this year he said it was time I really learned about the lens. It is a third order beehive Fresnel with six "bull's eyes". Grandpa said the word "order" really means size and that the U.S. Lighthouse Service has seven different orders of lens, 1st-6th including a 3-1/2 order. A first order is the biggest, over 12 feet tall and 6th the smallest, 18 inches or so high. Our third order is in the middle, about five feet high. These wonderful lenses were invented by a Frenchman, Augustine Fresnel, in 1823. Since they were much better than anything else available, they became an instant success and were soon used all over the world. Beehive refers to the shape of the lens. They kind of look like a beehive but I don't know any bees that would live in a glass house. The heavy glass lens prisms are all mounted in bronze frames, which are then bolted together. The prisms concentrate and focus the light from the lantern. Grandpa says the entire lens can be taken apart and carried away if necessary. I would like to see that sometime. Around the middle section of the lens are glass circles called bull's eyes. They focus the light into solid beams. If you were on top of the lens looking down, it would look like the spokes of a wagon wheel.

My job is to clean the glass every morning after the light is extinguished. I have to use a special cloth and cleaning fluid Grandpa keeps on the shelf in the watch room and put on a special linen apron. Grandpa will not take any chances of scratching the lens.

The lens has a little door in the back with brass hinges and a latch. It is actually part of

the lens. When you open it, you can reach a tall lantern located right in the middle of the lens. This is the lantern that provides the flame the lens magnifies for the ships. In the morning the lantern is carefully removed and carried down the stairs to the watch room below which has a little workbench. Grandpa sits at the workbench and carefully removes the glass chimney then uses a small pair of scissors to trim the cotton wick. He says many people call lightkeepers "wickies" because of the work they do trimming the wicks. He carefully cleans the lantern of black soot and fills the tank with oil making it ready for the next night. He has a second identical lamp ready too, just in case one does not work. He uses a set of special brass pitchers and measures to record exactly how much oil he uses, and writes the amount in a little leather book.

I almost forgot to tell you that as soon as we put the light out for the day, we have to lower the window shades. Grandpa said the sun can be so powerful, the lens can act like a big magnifying glass and actually cause a fire.

June 19

Today Grandma gave me a real surprise, my own lightkeepers uniform!

Grandpa of course has his official uniform, a dark blue suit with brass buttons. He only wears it when the Lighthouse Inspector makes an official visit or on Sundays when visitors come to the light. Normally he just works in regular clothes.

Before I came to the lighthouse, mother measured me up, but said she was planning to make me a new Sunday suit for Christmas, so I didn't think much of it. But she and Grandma must have been in "cahoots," because she sent the measurements to the lighthouse and Grandma had the uniform ready and waiting for me.

Grandma said, "Clothes make the man" and if I was going to work as a lightkeeper, I had to look like one too. I promised I would keep the uniform clean and only wear it when Grandpa wore his.

June 24

Today I learned about filling out the lighthouse log. It is really a journal, just like the one I am writing now. Everyday the keeper makes an entry and tells about the weather, number of ships that pass the light, what work he did that day and if anything important happens like a shipwreck or broken equipment.

Grandpa says it is very important that the log is filled out completely and neatly because when the inspector comes he will look at it very closely. Only the keeper can write in the log. I wish I could but he says that is one job I can't do.

June 27

This is a Sunday and a group of people from town came out to visit the lighthouse. Grandpa called them "tourists." It is a word I have not heard before. He says it means someone on vacation that wants to see everything there is to see. He was very nice to them and even took them up to the lens room and outside on the open galley. Some of the ladies were afraid to climb the stairs. I thought that was really funny. They arrived just as we were sitting down to supper but Grandpa still went out and greeted them very nicely. I would have been mad but he explained the Lighthouse Service says being nice to visitors is very important. He also said we have to be careful that the visitors do not break anything and that they are not allowed to touch the lens or machinery.

July 1

Grandma has a small garden behind the house. She started it when she came to the lighthouse about ten years ago and it has grown very large. She grows potatoes, corn, green beans and tomatoes. Grandma says it is very important to grow their own vegetables because they are so far from town and the tender only comes every three months.

Grandma will also "can" many of the vegetables, which will preserve them so they can have them during the winter. At the edge of the woods there is a small cave dug into the side of a hill with a door in front. This is called the root cellar and even on the hottest summer days it is cool inside. This is where they keep all of their perishable food. In town, the ice man comes and delivers big blocks of ice for our kitchen ice box but the lighthouse is too far away for such things. Grandpa says the root cellar is just fine.

They also have a grove of two dozen apple trees near the tower. In the fall Grandpa uses them to make apple cider and Grandma makes great apple pies. She always keeps a bushel or two of apples in the root cellar so I can have some during my summer visits.

Grandma also has Bessie the cow for milk and butter and a dozen chickens are in a coop behind the boathouse. I haven't milked Bessie yet but she says she will teach me soon.

July 4

Today is the 4th of July and we had great fun!

Grandpa said they always make it a special day, a
real celebration of our country's birthday and he
was right. We hurried through our regular jobs,
getting the light ready for sunset. There are no
holidays for lightkeepers. Our work still had to
be done.

About noon a large group of people from town
came out to the lighthouse with wagons and started
to set up for the annual party. The men dug a long fire
pit, about ten feet long, three feet wide and two feet
deep. They filled it with firewood and lit it. After a
couple of hours the wood had pretty well burned
down to a thick bed of glowing embers. Several of the
men placed large iron grills across the coals and some of the
women started cooking chicken over the fire. Others filled the grill with corn on
the cob still in the husks. I have never seen anything like it before, but Grandpa
said they do it every year. Other men made a table from long planks of wood laid
on saw horses. Women covered the table with red cloths. Several men unloaded

barrels of
root beer and
ginger ale from one of the
wagons and set them up under a shady tree. By
5:00 p.m. everything was ready and the table was piled with
heaps of grilled chicken, roasted corn and a dozen different kinds of pie and
cake. The food was great! I especially liked the chicken covered with a red
sauce one of the men called "barbecue" fixings! The root beer was good too
and Grandma warned me not to have too much of it or I would become sick.
Later we played horseshoes and had a three-legged sack race.

At sunset we lit the lantern for the Fresnel and it's powerful beams cut deep
into the black night. It was a great 4th of July.

July 10

Our lens of course is located at the top of the light tower. The focal plane, or center of the lens, is 100 feet above the water. Considering the curvature of the earth that we learned about in school, this means our light can be seen by a ship 14 miles away! The weather has to be perfect for it to be seen that far. If it is raining, foggy or snowing, you have to be much closer to see it.

To reach our lens, we climb a long, narrow spiral staircase that winds around and around inside the tower. When I was little, the stairs scared me but not any more. Yesterday I counted 141 steps to the top of the tower.

There are different kinds of light stations. Some lights are welcoming beacons intended to bring ships into a safe harbor. Our light is a warning beacon, letting sailors know about the dangerous reefs that are nearby and telling them to stay away.

The light tower is made of brick. Some towers are built of stone or rock and a few of wood, but Grandpa says brick is the best. Every year in early summer when the weather is calm, the tower has to be whitewashed. Usually Grandpa and his assistant do the job but this year since I am his assistant, I have to help. First Grandpa rigged a block and tackle set from the top of the tower to a small wooden seat he called a bosun's chair. It looks kind of like a seat on a swing. I sat in the seat and then he tied me down so I wouldn't fall out. He tied a can of whitewash to the chair, handed me a big paintbrush and said, "Hold on." He pulled on the rope and I lifted into the air. Was I scared! I shut both eyes tight, then slowly opened one, saw I was way up in the air so I shut it again. After a few minutes however, I opened them and realized I was okay. Grandpa shouted to me to start painting so I did, carefully painting the brick tower. When I finished one part of the tower, Grandpa either raised or lowered me so I could get to an unpainted part.

July 18

Today Grandpa told me that to a sailor the light from our lighthouse beam is different from any other lighthouse in the area. He called this a "characteristic." This way when a sailor sees our light, he will recognize it and know just where he is. Our lens rotates or turns to make our light look different from other lighthouses. For example, our lens rotates once every minute, giving six flashes during that time. Remember the bull's eyes I told you about before? Well they are what actually makes the flash. The lens is mounted on a huge, five-foot high iron base known as a pedestal. Inside is a complicated device with lots of gears called clockworks. It works just like a Grandpa's clock but much larger. A big crank on the side is wound up every four hours, which brings a heavy weight up inside the wall of the lighthouse. When it is released, the weight goes down and makes the clockworks move slowly, which in turn makes the big lens turn. It looks complicated but really is very simple. I tried winding it up today and it was hard but I was able to do it. Grandpa says I have a new job now!

Some lighthouses
have colored glass in
their lenses so when they
rotate, there are white flashes and
colored flashes. The next lighthouse to
the west flashes red for five seconds, then white
for ten, then red for five.

Our lighthouse also has a special daytime characteristic too. The tower is white with a black cap over the lens room and the keeper's quarters are made of red brick. When a sailor sees this color combination, he knows just where he is at any time. Our foghorn also has a special characteristic. It blows for five seconds, off for thirty and then back on for another five seconds. This is also different from any other lighthouse foghorn. Grandpa showed me a book called the "Coast Pilot" which listed all the lighthouses on the coast and their characteristics. There were hundreds of them, all different. These lighthouse men are very smart to be able to figure all of this out.

July 20

I had a very busy time last night. About midnight Grandma shook me awake and said to me, "Get up to the light tower, Grandpa needs your help." I quickly dressed and put a raincoat on since it was pouring "cat and dogs."

I ran up the steps to the watch room where I found Grandpa cranking the lens around by hand. He told me the wire holding the heavy clockworks weight broke and he could not fix it until morning. We would have to rotate the heavy lens by hand.

All night long we took turns cranking the lens. We worked an hour on and an hour off. It was hard work but the ships depended on our light and we couldn't fail them.

Twice during the night Grandma brought up cups of hot cocoa for me and coffee for Grandpa. It tasted so good and really helped keep me going.

When dawn finally came, we stopped and Grandpa went to work fixing the wire cable. By noon he had found the break and repaired it. Tonight we won't have to crank the lens by hand.

July 22

This morning I had a terrible job to do, shoveling dead birds off the outside walkway around the lens! There must have been a hundred of them! Grandpa says sometimes the bright light of the lens confuses the birds at night and they fly right into it, crashing into the glass windows of the lens room killing themselves.

Sometimes they hit so hard, they actually break the glass. Grandpa said it isn't all bad. Once just before Christmas a flock of geese smashed into the windows. That year they had goose for Christmas dinner!

Speaking of the windows, they are a lot of work too. Every morning I have to clean them both inside and outside. Grandpa says it is no good having a clean bright light if the beams can't get through dirty windows.

July 25

Today Grandpa noticed a
strange ship heading for the
lighthouse. After looking at it through
his big telescope, he told me that it was
a lighthouse tender and to "Tell your
Grandma the inspector's coming. She will
know what to do. Then hurry and sweep out the tower stairs and make sure the cans in the
oil house are polished and all lined up straight like I showed you. Now, get moving. There
is no time to waste!" I knew the inspector's job was to check all the lighthouses to make
certain they were all properly operated, but I had never actually seen a real inspector.

When I told Grandma what Grandpa said, she went right to work. She was a whirlwind!
The first thing she did was make an apple pie! This didn't make sense to me. What does
an apple pie have to do with an inspection? But I'll explain later. While the pie was
baking, she started cleaning up the house. Grandma kept everything very clean, so I didn't
understand what she had left to do. She said, "No matter how clean something is, it is
never clean enough for an inspector."

I quickly swept the tower and straightened the oil room. Grandpa went up to the lens
room to make certain everything was shipshape. After about an hour Grandpa and I
walked down to the dock just as the boat from the tender arrived. A large man in a
uniform similar to Grandpa's stepped on to the dock and said, "Hello Frank, I know you

are ready for my inspection. You always are. Is this the young man you told me about?" Grandpa then introduced me to the inspector and we shook hands. He was taller than my Grandpa and had a big bushy moustache.

The inspector checked the light tower very carefully, especially the lens and clockworks. He had a pair of white gloves and ran a finger all around the lens looking for dirt and dust. Grandpa was very proud that he didn't find any. I was proud too since it was my job to keep the lens clean. Then he inspected the oil house, boathouse and fog house, making sure everything was clean and in its right place.

He checked the quarters too, peering under beds looking for dust and opening all the closets and kitchen cabinets to make sure that everything was in order. Finally he sat down at the kitchen table and Grandma gave him a cup of coffee and a thick slice of apple pie warm out of the oven. We all sat down too and had pie. I had a glass of lemonade. The inspector said, "Frank, your inspection is perfect again. You really do a great job keeping this light. And Ethel (which was my Grandma's name) your apple pie is the best I ever had. You know it's my

favorite." Grandpa winked at Grandma when he heard that but the inspector never saw the wink. Grandpa said, "Well, a lot of credit should go to my grandson. He is doing an excellent job as my assistant." When I heard that, I felt like I was ten feet tall!

At the dock, the tender crew had finished unloading our supplies. There were large barrels of oil for the lanterns, 100-pound bags of coal for the fog signal and a whole pile of smaller boxes of other supplies. We would have a lot of work to put it all away. When the inspector rowed back to the tender, he waved back at us and said, "Keep up the good work. I'll be back in a couple of months."

July 29

Today I learned all about the fuel we used in the lanterns. We always just call it oil, but Grandpa explained that there were different kinds. He said originally the keepers used whale oil, usually from the sperm whale. But so many Yankee whale ships were sunk during the Civil War by the Confederates, they started to run out of it and the price went very high, too high for the Lighthouse Service to afford it. So the government looked for other fuels. For a while they tried Calzola oil, which was made from cabbages, but it wasn't very good. Finally he said they settled on Mineral oil, which was invented by the Canadians and made from oil pumped from the ground. Some people call it kerosene. It is very flammable and we need to be very careful with it. Mineral oil also burns very bright, so it is very good for lighthouse use.

August 1

One of the things I miss living at the lighthouse is the town library. I enjoy reading so much it is hard to give it up for the summer.

I was really surprised to discover that the lighthouse has a library too. The books are kept in a wood box about three feet wide, three feet tall and a foot deep. It has two doors with a hasp lock across the front. The collection of books is very good. There are about 50 in the box and they include volumes on gardening, cooking, history, fiction, just about everything you could want to read. I especially like the books written by Mark Twain.

Every three months the tender brings a new library box and takes the old one. This way the libraries are constantly changed between the light stations. A new library box was left by the tender when it brought the inspector.

August 6

One of the books in the box is about lighthouses all around the world. It is very interesting and I learned things I never knew before. The first lighthouse was built in Alexandria, Egypt in the third century BC, that is about 2200 years ago! It was a huge tower, hundreds of feet tall and was called Pharos. Eventually the tower was destroyed by an earthquake. Before Pharos people burned bonfires on the beach to help guide sailors to safety.

The Romans built many lighthouses, at least 30 according to the book.

During the Middle Ages maritime countries like England, Denmark, Italy and Germany built many small light towers along their shores. They didn't have lenses like we do today. Instead open fires were burned on the tops of the towers. I guess it was better than nothing. Later they used a complicated system of lamp and reflectors.

The first lighthouse in the U.S. was constructed in 1716 at Little Brewster Island near Boston. Before the American Revolution there were a dozen lights along the Atlantic coast.

Once we won the Revolution, shipping activity greatly increased and more and more lighthouses were built. Today we have hundreds of lighthouses, spread out on the Atlantic, Pacific and Great Lakes coasts.

The book also told about lenses and other equipment and had lots of stories of famous lighthouse keepers. I am anxious to finish reading it. Books are so much fun!

August 12

Today we visited my Uncle Dan down at Rocky Point, about four miles to the east. He is the keeper of the U.S. Life-Saving Station. I had been there once three or four years ago but do not remember much about the visit. If a ship wrecks nearby, he has to take his crew out and try to save the people aboard. He has eight men called surfmen at the station. Each man has a number, one–eight. The number one surfman is the most experienced and number eight the newest man.

The crew has two special boats. One is a surfboat, about 26 feet long. The crew launches it into the waves from a small wagon then rows out and makes the rescue. This is a very difficult thing to do during a storm.

The other is a bigger boat, called a lifeboat. It is about 34 feet long and very heavy. It is made to batter through the waves and is considered unsinkable. It can only be launched from a special ramp at the station boathouse.

Twice a week Uncle Dan takes his crew out in the boats and they actually roll them over and then right them again. He told me they have to practice it because they could roll over during a rescue and would have to be able to right them.

They also have a little bronze cannon they call a Lyle gun. It is used to shoot a line from the beach to sailors on a wreck. The sailors use the line to pull a larger rope out and eventually rig what they call a "breeches buoy" from ship to shore. One at a time the sailors can ride it to safety far above the waves. It is all very complicated and although I have watched the life-savers practice it, I can't explain it in detail.

There also is a tall lookout tower and Uncle Dan said there is a life-saver on watch 24 hours a day, keeping a sharp eye for shipwrecks. If he sees one, he rings a bell and the crew goes to the rescue. During the night another surfman patrols the beach for four miles in each direction. If he sees a wreck, he burns a red flare as a signal, which is seen by the tower lookout who rings the alarm bell to call the life-saving crew.

Grandpa told me the life-savers have a special motto. "Regulations say we have to go out. They don't say anything about coming back." He also said entire life-saving crews have been lost trying to make rescues. In the newspapers his men are sometimes called Storm Warriors or Heroes of the Surf. Last November Uncle Dan's crew rescued 12 men from a sinking schooner in the middle of a terrible storm. I think they are the bravest men I have ever seen. Nothing ever scares them.

August 19

Well, my time at the lighthouse is almost finished and soon I will be going back home. I am anxious to see my family again. As much as I love my grandparents, I do miss my family. I will also be back in school too and I hope my teacher likes this journal. I tried to keep a good record of everything that happened, it has been fascinating and I have learned a lot.

August 20

This morning Grandpa said there would be a big storm coming. He can tell because his barometer is falling. I learned about how barometers can help forecast the weather in school last year. About noon a whole line of black clouds came boiling in from the west accompanied by thunder and lightning. It was so dark, it looked like night. By sunset rain was falling in buckets and the waves were rolling very high. They were the largest I have ever seen and hit the rocks with a tremendous crash. When we went to bed the wind was blowing so hard I thought the tower would blow right over! Just before dark, our chicken coop blew away. There was just a big swoosh and it was gone. I guess there will not be any eggs for breakfast.

August 21

This was the most exciting day I have ever had! All night long the storm blew and blew. Thunder crashed so close I thought the roof would collapse. In the morning the wind was so strong I nearly blew away when I went to the light tower. As I climbed the stairs, I felt the tower shaking from the blasts of wind. The view from the top was incredible. Everywhere the water was white with foam. The sound the wind made as it whistled through the lens room almost hurt my ears. Suddenly Grandpa grabbed my arm and pointed off to the west. About three miles away I saw a schooner wrecked on Ripper Rocks. Enormous waves were breaking right over the ship and I was certain it would smash into pieces any minute. Between the ship and shore was a small white boat slowly

rowing out toward the wreck. The waves were huge and the little boat disappeared when they swept over it, then it reappeared and kept on going. It was Uncle Dan's lifeboat! The life-savers were going out to make a rescue.

Grandpa pointed off to the east. I saw a small boat with two men in it. It was the schooner's yawl and the wind had almost blown it into the breakers along the beach. Certainly it would overturn in the waves drowning the men before they could reach shore. The life-savers were too far away to help. Grandpa and I ran down the stairs to the boathouse where we each took a long coil of rope and a life jacket. Then we ran along the beach until we were near where the boat would wash ashore. Grandpa put a life jacket on me and tied a rope around my waist. He tied a loop in the second rope and told me, "When they roll over in the surf, run into the waves and throw a rope to them. I will hold the other end and keep you from being swept away. Then I will haul you both ashore. This is a man's job, but there is no one else and I know you can do it!" I was too busy to be scared. I just knew I had to try to save these men. The boat soon tumbled in the surf and the men were thrown into the crashing waves. I quickly ran into the water dragging the ropes behind me. A big wave knocked me over, but I got up and kept trying to fight my way out to the men. Finally I was close enough to throw the rope. One man grabbed it and Grandpa pulled us both to the beach.

As I was bending over with my hands on my knees trying to catch my breath, I heard a familiar voice. "Johnny, you saved my life!" It was my teacher, Miss Swenson." The "man" I had thrown the rope to was Miss Swenson! I wanted to ask her a hundred questions, but Grandpa said, "No time for that now. Let's try to find the other fellow." We looked for the second man but he had disappeared in the waves.

Grandpa, Miss Swenson and I trudged up the beach and back to our house. Grandma gave Miss Swenson some dry clothes and fed her hot tea and toast slathered with apple preserves. Grandpa and I changed clothes too, then had hot coffee. He said, "You did a man's work today and should have a man's drink." He drank his black, but I added sugar and cream to mine.

Slowly Miss Swenson explained how she ended up on the shipwreck. "Johnny, you remember the assignment I gave the class for the summer, to keep a journal of your adventures?" I nodded my head. "Well," she said, "I thought I should have an adventure too, so I dressed in man's clothes and took passage on the schooner for South Point City. I knew the captain would not take a woman on board, so my disguise was necessary. I didn't plan on a shipwreck!" I asked her, "But why didn't you wait for the life-savers?" She said, "When we hit the rocks, the mate panicked and launched the small boat. I was confused about what to do, so he told me to get into it and before I knew what was happening we capsized in the waves. The next thing I remember was you throwing me the rope." Miss Swenson looked so worn out Grandma put her right to bed.

Although Grandma didn't say much, I could tell she was very angry with Grandpa for having me go out into the water with the rope. But I think he was right. She still thinks I am a little boy. If he had gone into the water, I was not strong enough to pull him back, let alone a survivor too!

I later found out Uncle Dan and his life-saving crew saved all of the sailors on the wreck. The Storm Warriors had come through again!

August 25

Dad came and picked me up today. I said goodbye to my grandparents and thanked them for letting me stay all summer. It was a great adventure. Grandpa said I could be his assistant anytime. Uncle Dan even came over from the life-saving station to say goodbye too. He told everybody that he had heard how brave I was during the storm and said he would be proud to have me as a member of his crew, but I would have to wait until I was 18 years old to join the life-savers. Maybe I can spend next summer with him and his crew. That would be really exciting!

The biggest surprise of all was that Uncle Dan brought Miss Swenson with him and announced they were going to be married! He said, "I've known Katrina for a long time but she would never marry me because of my job as a life-saver. She said it was too dangerous and wanted me to take a job ashore. But after her experience last week being shipwrecked and saved, she said she finally understood how important my job was and she agreed to be my wife."

I can't wait to show her my journal!